Anna Hibiscus

ANNA HIBISCUS

Atinuke

illustrated by Lauren Tobia

CANDLEWICK PRESS

Text copyright © 2010, 2022 by Atinuke
Illustrations copyright © 2010, 2022 by Lauren Tobia

First Candlewick Press edition 2022
First US edition published by Kane Miller 2010
First published by Walker Books (UK) 2007

Library of Congress Catalog Card Number 2021946698
ISBN 978-1-5362-2519-8 (hardcover)
ISBN 978-1-5362-2523-5 (paperback)

22 23 24 25 26 27 LBM 10 9 8 7 6 5 4 3 2 1

Printed in Melrose Park, IL, USA

This book was typeset in Stempel Schneider and Lauren.
The illustrations were done in ink.

Candlewick Press
99 Dover Street
Somerville, Massachusetts 02144

www.candlewick.com

For the children of Fachongle
A

For Paul, Lizzie, and Alice,
my family and friends
LT

Anna Hibiscus on Holiday

Anna Hibiscus lives in Africa. Amazing
Africa. In a country called Nigeria.

She lives in an old white house with
balconies and secret staircases. A wonderful
house in a beautiful garden inside a big
compound. The trees are full of sweet ripe
fruit and the flowers are full of sweet juicy
nectar because this is Africa, and Africa can
be like this. Outside the compound is the
city. An amazing city of lagoons and bridges
and roads, of skyscrapers and shantytowns.

Anna Hibiscus lives with her mother, who is from Canada; her father, who is from Africa; her grandmother and her grandfather; her aunties and her uncles; lots and lots of cousins; and her twin baby brothers, Double and Trouble.

There are so many people in Anna's family that even she cannot count them all.

Anna Hibiscus is never lonely. There are always cousins to play and fight with, uncles and aunties are always laughing and shouting, and her mother or father and grandmother and grandfather are always around.

To be alone in Anna Hibiscus's house, you have to hide. Sometimes Anna squeezes into some cool, dusty, forgotten place and waits for that exciting moment when her family begins to call—and then a cousin or uncle finds her and her aunties thank God!

One day, Anna's mother told the family that in Canada she grew up in a house with only her mother and her father.

"What!" cried Auntie Grace. "All alone? Only the three of you?"

"Yes, and I had a room all of my own," Anna's mother said wistfully.

Anna's grandmother looked at her. "Dey made you sleep alone?" she asked.

"It was not a punishment," Anna's mother said. "It was a good thing to have my own room."

Anna Hibiscus and her cousins looked at each other. Imagine! Sleeping alone. Alone in the dark!

"Nobody likes to sleep alone," said Anna's grandmother.

Anna Hibiscus laid her warm brown cheek on her mother's white arm. "Don't worry, Mama," she said. "You have all of us now. You will never be alone again."

But the next week, Anna's father said, "Anna Hibiscus, we are going on holiday. Your mother and myself with you and those brothers of yours. We will stay in a house on the beach."

"Only us?" asked Anna. This was incredible.

"Only us," said her father. "A quiet holiday."

Anna Hibiscus's mother smiled.

"But, Papa," said Anna, "who is going to cook and shop and clean and . . . everything? Who will take care of Double Trouble? What about me? Who will I play with?"

"I will help your mother to organize everything," Anna's father told her. "You, Anna Hibiscus, will take care of your brothers. You can play with them."

"But they are babies!" wailed Anna.

"Exactly!" said her father. "Now, enough problems. Let us pack."

One week later, Anna Hibiscus, her father, her mother, Double and Trouble, *and* all their boxes and bags crossed the road to the lagoon and squeezed themselves into a small canoe. The whole family waved them off.

"Don' stay long!" they shouted. "Come soon!"

The lagoon ran under and alongside busy roads and huge skyscrapers; it ran through markets bigger than towns. For the first time, Anna Hibiscus saw how big the city was. It was gigantic.

Then it was gone.

Suddenly it was not buildings but trees that crowded the banks of the lagoon. Trees so tall and growing so thick together that Anna could not see into the dark rain forest. Only once did she see some people, looking tiny, on the bank.

Morning turned into afternoon turned into evening as they went slowly-slowly. Then Anna could see the island! A white sandy beach with small trees and, behind them, an open wooden house, painted white.

It was late by the time they got all their boxes and bags off the boat and up to the beach house. Anna Hibiscus's father lit lanterns, and her mother warmed up food. They were all so tired from breathing sea breezes and carrying boxes and bags that they went straight to bed. Even Double and Trouble slept right through till morning.

When Anna and her family woke up,
the beach house seemed dusty and dirty.
It was full of cobwebs and dead cockroaches.
Their boxes and bags were still packed. They
were hungry. There was a lot to do.

After breakfast, Anna was put in charge of
Double Trouble. They stayed downstairs on
the veranda, where it was cool and shady,
but the boys kept crawling toward the edge.
There were no doors for Anna to shut. She
ran backward and forward, grabbing each of
her brothers in turn and putting them back
in the middle of the room.

She was hot and sweating when at last
she attached the boys to a table leg

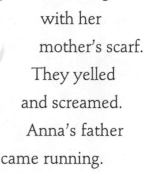

with her
mother's scarf.
They yelled
and screamed.
Anna's father
came running.

"Anna Hibiscus!" he
said. "They are not goats!"

He untied them and
watched them crawl quickly
toward the
edge of
the veranda.

"I see."
He sighed.
"Double Trouble!"

He called to Anna's mother.

"I'm taking Anna Hibiscus and Double
Trouble to the beach. Where they cannot
fall off any edge."

Anna's mother
appeared in the
kitchen doorway.

There was a smudge on
her face and cobwebs in
her hair.

"OK," she sighed.

At the beach, the boys wanted to crawl into the sea. The waves shot up their noses and splashed salt water in their eyes. They spluttered and choked and coughed.

Anna's father took them to play under the trees. "You go and splash yourself, Anna Hibiscus," he said. "I will stay here with your brothers."

Anna was not at all sure about splashing in the sea by herself. What if one of those big waves came along and drowned her? There would be no uncle or auntie to save her.

She put
one toe in the
water, but there were
no cousins to be brave with.

Anna Hibiscus could hear Double
and Trouble shouting and struggling.
They wanted to crawl back into the water.
They were not afraid.

Anna's father dug a big hole in the sand.
Big enough for Double and Trouble to sit in
and play. Too deep for the boys to climb out.

"You stay with them now, Anna,"
said her father. "I am going to swim."

Double and Trouble cried and screamed.
They rubbed sand into their eyes and
screamed louder. Anna sat with them
in the hole. Her father's head
was a black ball
in the waves.

A black ball
getting smaller and smaller.
Just before it disappeared, it began to
grow big again. Anna's father swam
back with an idea.

He and Anna Hibiscus lifted the boys
out of the hole and pointed them in the
direction of the sea. Anna and her father
ran down to the waves with Double
Trouble crawling eagerly behind them.

They had time to splash and swim
a little before the boys reached
the water. Then Anna
and her father
helped them
paddle before
carrying
them back
up to the
trees to start
again. Double
Trouble loved it!
Anna Hibiscus and
her father did this many,
many, many times—until they
were too tired to do it anymore.

Back at the beach house, Anna Hibiscus's mother was tired too. She had swept up all the cockroaches. She had dusted away all the cobwebs. She had unpacked all the boxes and bags. She had walked all the way to the market to buy food and walked all the way back. She had cooked the food.

Everybody was cranky and tired. Everybody was hot and sticky. Everybody had a shower, ate food, and went to bed early. Everybody was asleep in one second.

Half an hour later, Double and Trouble woke up.

They were again hot and sticky. Their
teeth were paining them. They were Awake
and Angry. Anna Hibiscus's mother and
father walked the baby boys up
and down for hours while they
screamed.

Anna Hibiscus lay
in her bed. She
had nobody
to sleep
with.

She missed her
aunties. She missed how they
took it in turns to rock sleepless babies.
She missed how they sang and talked and
made jokes and laughed no matter how
loud the babies cried. Now Anna could hear
only the waves and her brothers, screaming.

The next morning, Anna Hibiscus's father was so tired he could hardly speak. Anna Hibiscus's mother was so tired she cried. The boys were Full of Life! They crawled everywhere, fast. Double pulled the tablecloth, and cups of tea spilled and rolled off the table onto the floor. Trouble crawled off the veranda and landed with a big bump on his head.

Anna's mother said,
"I can't face it."

"You don't have
to face it," Anna's
father said. And
he sent her
back to bed.

He watched
Anna trying
to stop her
brothers from
crawling off the veranda.
He remembered yesterday.
He could not face it either.

Anna Hibiscus's father found the
scarf and attached Double Trouble to
the table leg. He set Anna to watch them.

"I go come," he said.

"Where?" asked Anna.

"I go to fetch aunties quick-quick," he said.
Anna Hibiscus smiled a big smile.

Later that morning, the aunties arrived.
Six of them. They came with baskets of
food. They came with little cousins who
still needed them but no big cousins. They
came with cuddles for Anna Hibiscus and
many, many questions. When they saw
Double and Trouble attached to the table
leg, they shouted and ran to free them.
Each boy was tied onto an auntie's back to
keep him out of mischief. They went into
the kitchen and started to cook. Good
smells spread all around, along with
laughing and singing.

Anna's mother woke up. She stood blinking at the top of the stairs. She looked as if she did not know whether to laugh or to cry.

"Sister!" one of the aunties called. "Our brother confused your babies with the goats and tied them to the table!"

Anna's mother started to laugh *and* to cry. She came to greet the aunties. They embraced her.

"It is not good to be alone," Anna heard them whisper. "We have to help each other. A husband and three children is too much for one woman alone."

That night, everybody was happy.

The next day, the aunties and Anna Hibiscus's mother cooked and cleaned and washed clothes because they needed to. They splashed in the sea and sat talking on the beach because they were on holiday. They sang and joked because they were together.

And all the time, the little cousins were under their feet. Anna Hibiscus tried to play with them, but they were babies and she could not look after them all. There were no big cousins to distract them and no one else for them to follow around. The little cousins whined and howled. They grizzled and growled. Because that's what little children do. Anna Hibiscus was fed up with them.

By the end of the day, the aunties and Anna Hibiscus's mother had had enough.

Back at the beach house, they looked at Anna's father. "Today you sit down," they said. "Tomorrow you supervise this rabble!"

Anna Hibiscus's father looked at the rabble. He'd had a lovely quiet day eating the delicious food that the women had prepared and reading his newspapers. The rabble was snotty and sticky and cranky. They scratched one another and pulled each other's hair.

"Tomorrow I will be here," he said. Then he quickly walked out of the house and disappeared down toward the beach.

Tomorrow he *was* there. He was there, and all the big cousins that had been left behind were there to help him.

Anna's father supervised the big cousins supervising the little cousins over the top of his newspaper. The aunties and Anna's mother laughed and sighed and shook their heads.

Anna Hibiscus splashed and swam and ran and played with all her cousins. It was the best day so far.

That night, the women talked and joked together. The babies slept. The big cousins played their big-cousin games. Anna's father sat alone. He had no one to discuss the newspapers with, no one to smoke his pipe with. Anna came and laid her cheek on his knee.

"I am outnumbered, Anna Hibiscus," he said.

"You need the uncles," she said.

The next
morning, the uncles
were there! The women
shrieked with surprise
and laughed.
Anna's father
looked very pleased
with himself.
It was another
good day and
another good
night.

But there came a day when everybody was annoyed and irritated. Nobody could agree. Anna's mother looked at Anna's father. He disappeared down toward the beach.

When he returned, Grandmother and Grandfather were with him. Grandmother and Grandfather had lived so long, they had become so wise and so calm that anybody who was with them was happy to accept their last word on everything. There was no need to quarrel. Harmony was restored.

Anna Hibiscus splashed in the sea with her big cousins; she chased her little cousins along the beach; she sang with her aunties and ate their good food; she laughed with her uncles and her father. She listened to Grandmother and Grandfather tell stories.

All together again, Anna Hibiscus's family
had the happiest holiday they had ever had.

And Anna's mother?
She had a very happy
holiday too.

Auntie Comfort

Anna Hibiscus lives in Africa. Amazing
Africa. In a country called Nigeria.

She lives in a big white house with many
rooms and balconies. She lives with her
family, who does things the African way.
Grandmother and Grandfather, who are very
old and very wise, say it is important to do
things the proper African way.

All of Anna Hibiscus's family—her mother
and her father, her aunties and her uncles,
her cousins and Anna herself—bend their
knees to Grandmother and Grandfather and
the other elders to show proper respect for
their wisdom and their age.

Anna's big cousins
go to school and university,
but they also work hard at home
helping to wash the clothes, cook the food,
and look after the little cousins.

Anna's mother and father and aunties
and uncles drive to work in their cars. They
send text messages and emails around the
world and call from the market on their cell
phones to see what shopping needs doing.
But the clothes they wear are made from
colorful African cloth, waxed and dyed
and printed. The languages they speak are
African as well as English.

Even Anna Hibiscus's mother, who is from Canada, does things the proper African way. Anna has seen her in photos, when she was young, wearing a bikini. Now she wears buba and wrappa like the aunties—and has a suitable swimsuit like they do.

When Anna's mother comes home from the office, she pounds yam and cassava in the yard with the aunties. She cooks traditional food the traditional way— and she knows how to eat it properly with her fingers too!

You see, the whole family does things the proper African way, both modern and traditional. That is why Anna's grandmother and grandfather, her mother and her father, her aunties and her uncles, her cousins and her baby brothers—and Anna herself—all live together in the big white house.

All except for Auntie Comfort.

Auntie Comfort is one of Anna Hibiscus's favorite questions, especially on the Saturday Beach.

"Where is Auntie Comfort?"

"I've told you many, many times, Anna Hibiscus," her mother says, sighing.

"Tell me again, Mama, please," Anna begs.

"Again! Again!" all the little cousins shout.

And all the aunties sigh.

"You children will tire us!" they say.

But Uncle Tunde, who is not yet married and has no children and is not so tired of questions, says, "Auntie Comfort is in America."

"Where? Where?" Anna Hibiscus and all the little cousins shout.

Uncle Tunde points. "Over these same waves. On the other side of the Atlantic Ocean." He shades his eyes. "I can almost see her from here."

And they all jump up and try to see Auntie Comfort across the ocean.

Once, Anna was so excited she ran right down to the waves.

"Maybe one day, when you are strong enough," called Auntie Grace, "you will swim right across the Atlantic Ocean to Auntie Comfort!"

"Am I almost strong enough?" Anna Hibiscus said seriously.

Everybody laughed and laughed. Anna didn't know why they were laughing at her. She wanted to cry.

"Come," said Anna's mother, who was in a good mood. "Let us send her a text message across the ocean instead!"

She showed Anna and the little cousins how to send a text message to Auntie Comfort. Anna pointed the cell phone toward the waves and sent the message all the way across the Atlantic Ocean.

The next day was Sunday. On Sunday the whole family goes to church wearing special traditional clothes cut from the one same beautiful cloth to show they are all from the one same beautiful family.

Grandfather was proud of his family. He was happy that his sons were big and laughing. It pleased him that his daughters were strong and happy. He loved his grandchildren, full of life and trouble.

He looked at Grandmother, whose wise eyes were full of love, and he loved her too.

Only Comfort was missing. His youngest daughter. His comfort. Tears came suddenly into Grandfather's eyes. Anna Hibiscus, who was standing close to him, saw his tears. What could be troubling Grandfather? He was so old and wise. Nothing should be allowed to trouble Grandfather! Anna Hibiscus went to him and put her hand in his.

The next day, a letter came. A letter from Auntie Comfort!

"Praise God!" said Grandfather when he had read it. "Comfort will visit us at last!"

Tears streamed down Grandmother's and Grandfather's cheeks. Aunties and uncles and cousins jumped up and down, smiling and clapping and shouting, "Comfort is coming! Auntie Comfort is coming!"

"In three weeks' time," Grandfather continued, "Comfort will return on holiday."

And for three weeks, everybody—little, medium, and big—was busy working in preparation for Auntie Comfort's visit. When she came, every day would be a party.

Benz, Wonderful, and all the big boy cousins led home from market goats carefully chosen by Grandfather and the uncles. They had to keep those goats tied up and eating.

Miracle, Sweetheart, and all the little girl cousins were busy every day feeding the chickens fattening in pens.

The big gas stove in the kitchen was not big enough to prepare all the food.

Anna, Chocolate, Angel, and all the medium-sized cousins were kept busy collecting wood to feed the fires. Pots bubbled and boiled, and Anna's mother and aunties stirred and sweated and strained.

Joy, Clarity, Common Sense, and all the big girl cousins grew muscles in their arms from pounding and pounding yam and cassava and millet.

Uncle Bizi Sunday, who was in charge of shopping and cooking and eating, did not sleep—not at all.

Soon the big fridges and freezers were stuffed full of delicious food and soft drinks, all waiting for Auntie Comfort to arrive.

But every evening when the family gathered to eat, a tear would run down Grandfather's cheek. He would look around at his wife and children and grandchildren, all rolling balls of yam neatly between their fingertips and popping them in their mouths.

"Will Comfort remember how to eat?" he would say. "Will she remember our way? The proper African way? Will she have forgotten her fingers and know only knife and fork now?"

The aunties and uncles would look at one another and smile and shrug their shoulders. They did not know. Only Anna Hibiscus was worried that Grandfather was sad again.

One night she asked her mother, "Mama, can I send a message on your phone?"

"What are you talking about, Anna Hibiscus?" her mother said, cranky and tired. "To who? Cell phones are not for children."

Uncle Tunde heard. He saw Anna's tears. Uncle Tunde had not been cooking all afternoon, and he was not so tired.

"Don't worry, Anna Hibiscus," he said. "You can use my phone."

So Anna sent a message across the Atlantic Ocean, and only Uncle Tunde knew.

In those three weeks before Auntie Comfort came, much new cloth was bought and new clothes made for the whole family. A lot of text messages were sent back and forth between the cloth market and the house. Auntie Comfort emailed her measurements, and the tailor came on his bicycle, his sewing machine strapped on the back, to help with the making of the new clothes. Grandmother called Grandfather to inspect each fitting. Grandfather sighed and shook his head when they held up Auntie Comfort's new clothes. "But will Comfort even know how to tie wrappa anymore? The proper African way? Maybe she will only wear tight-tight jean now."

Angel and Chocolate and Anna Hibiscus
looked at one another with eyes wide
open. An auntie wearing tight-tight jean!
The boy cousins giggled. The uncles
laughed. Grandmother looked worried.

Anna Hibiscus borrowed Uncle Tunde's
phone again.

The three weeks were almost gone. Anna was excited. Whenever she could, she ran off to play at being Auntie Comfort. Auntie Comfort in the office with many secretaries sending important emails and faxes around the world. All the cousins loved to play this game. On the last day, they played Auntie Comfort shopping for their presents!

Grandfather came out to watch. He shook his head.

"It is the proper African way to bring gifts for everyone," he said. "Maybe Auntie Comfort will not remember."

The cousins looked at one another.
Now they were *all* worried.

Anna Hibiscus went running to Uncle
Tunde. But it was too late! Too late for
Auntie Comfort to go shopping—Auntie
Comfort was coming tomorrow!

The next day, Anna Hibiscus's father and Uncle Tunde drove to the airport to collect Auntie Comfort.

The family stood on the porch in their new clothes. They watched and waited.

When Anna's father and Uncle Tunde returned, they were smiling from ear to ear. And when Auntie Comfort stepped out of the car, everybody gasped.

She was wearing the biggest, longest, fullest, stiffest traditional dress that Anna and her cousins had ever seen. It was a miracle that her head tie had fit inside the car!

Auntie Comfort looked like a queen. The Queen of Africa! Uncle Tunde winked at Anna.

When Auntie Comfort knelt in front of Grandmother and Grandfather, Anna Hibiscus thought she was the finest queen she had ever seen.

Anna's mother and all the aunties were crying with joy and relief. Anna's father and the uncles were laughing and smiling. Grandfather's smile was the happiest smile of all. And Anna Hibiscus's was the widest.

"Welcome, Comfort!" Grandfather said.

"Thank you, Father," Auntie Comfort replied. "But I am now called Yemisi."

"Why?"
said Grandmother.
"What is wrong with Comfort?"

"I wanted to have an African name,
Mama," said Auntie Comfort.

The aunties started to laugh.

"Comfort is an African name," said
Grandmother.

"But it is an English word, Mama," said
Auntie Comfort.

"It is an English word, but an African
name," said Grandfather. "Have you ever
heard of any English person being called
Comfort? Come, enough of this. Let us eat."

The table had been laid according to Grandfather's instructions. There were plates at every place, and many knives and forks and spoons, for the many courses. They ate pepper soup with their spoons, and then eba and okro and stew were served. Everybody looked at Auntie Comfort. Auntie Comfort looked politely at Grandmother and Grandfather.

Grandfather gestured to Auntie Comfort. "Begin, my daughter," he said.

Auntie Comfort motioned for the finger-washing bowl to be passed to her. Then she began. Rolling the eba into neat little balls with her fingertips, dipping it into the okro and stew, and then popping it into her mouth.

The cousins clapped and clapped. Big fat happy tears ran down Grandmother's and Grandfather's cheeks. Auntie Comfort looked surprised . . . and then she winked at Anna Hibiscus. Anna Hibiscus smiled her biggest smile.

The worry was over. Except . . .

What was inside Auntie
Comfort's many big suitcases?
Presents, of course!
There were presents for
Grandmother and
Grandfather, Mother
and Father and all the
aunties and uncles, *and* there
were presents for Anna,
Double Trouble, Benz,
Wonderful, Miracle,
Sweetheart, Chocolate,
Angel, Joy, Clarity,
Common Sense, and all of the
cousins. Everybody cried with
excitement and hugged Auntie Comfort
over and over again. Nobody
had been forgotten! Not
the neighbors, not
the distant relatives,
not the girls who

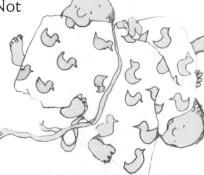

stood selling fruit and vegetables at the gate. Nobody.

Anna was delighted. Auntie Comfort had thought of everything and everyone.

After that, everybody, including Anna Hibiscus, knew that Auntie Comfort was still a true and proper African lady, both modern and traditional.

"Our daughter has come," Grandmother said over and over again.

"Our daughter has not only come," Grandfather said. "She has also remained one of us."

And everybody agreed.

Lucky, though, thought Anna Hibiscus when Auntie Comfort went splashing in the waves in a tiny-tiny bikini— lucky Grandmother and Grandfather don't come to the beach!

Anna Hibiscus Sells Oranges

Anna Hibiscus lives in Africa. Amazing
Africa. In the country of Nigeria.

She and her family live in a big white
house in a beautiful garden in the middle of
a compound. All around the compound is
a wide white wall. Outside the wall is
the city.

It is a big African city of lagoons and bridges and roads, of skyscrapers and shantytowns. Ships and boats sail up and down the lagoons, which wind through the city from the sea to the rain forest. Ships and boats loaded with people and goats and goods. Every road is jammed with hundreds and thousands of cars, buses, taxis, and motorbikes, all loaded with people and all blowing their horns.

There are millions and millions of people in Anna Hibiscus's city: people being born and people dying, people growing up and people growing old, people studying and people working, working, working. People walking, running, driving; singing, talking, shouting; laughing and fighting; buying and selling. The city is always busy and noisy and loud.

However noisy the city was, inside Anna Hibiscus's compound it was quiet, quiet, quiet. Auntie Comfort had flown back across the Atlantic Ocean to America. The days-long parties were over. The distant relatives had returned to their villages, and the neighbors had gone home. The big cousins were at school, and aunties and uncles were at work.

There were now only the daytime sounds of little cousins playing and a few aunties, sometimes singing, sometimes scolding. There were now only the evening sounds of uncles laughing and discussing. Sometimes only the murmur of Grandmother's and Grandfather's soft words could be heard.

Anna Hibiscus was bored of this quiet. She was bored of playing with her cousins, bored of housework with her mother, bored of listening quietly to Grandmother and Grandfather.

Anna loved to stand at the gate and watch the city. She knew all the girls who stood outside the gate selling fruit and vegetables from baskets piled high on their heads. She knew the women who squatted in the road frying plantains and braiding hair for money. She knew the small boys who sold matches. They all called and sang to the people passing on foot, or in cars and buses and bikes: "COME AN' BUY! COME AN' BUY!"

Anna loved the girls who
sold oranges and plantains
the most. Whole busloads
of people stopped to buy
their oranges. Motorbikes
pulled over for plantains.
Those girls shouted
and screamed and laughed
and talked to everybody.
They ran after passing
cars for money held out of
opened windows. They
fought off goats who ate the
plantains. They chased
off children who stole their
oranges. The girls at the
gate did not have to play
boring games with little
cousins all day long. They
were busy with the whole
city. Those girls did not look bored.

Many, many times Anna Hibiscus
asked her mother and her father,
her grandmother and her
grandfather, "Abeg, Papa,
please can I go out? I
want to sell oranges
at the gate."

But Grandfather
always laughed.

"Ah-ah, Anna
Hibiscus, why do you
want to sell oranges?
You are a lucky girl.
You have a father and a
mother who work for you.
Even I, when I was young, worked
for you: for our beautiful big white house,
for our garden, where you can play and
pick fruit anytime you like. Go and play,
Anna Hibiscus; you do not know how lucky
you are!"

One day Anna Hibiscus was so bored she decided not to listen to Grandfather. She decided to sell oranges anyway.

Anna found a big basket. She climbed one of the orange trees and filled it full of fruit. Then she slipped out of the gate with her basket on her head.

"Orrrr-enge! Orrrr-enge!" Anna Hibiscus shouted just like the other girls. They all looked at her with surprised and worried eyes.

Anna Hibiscus's oranges were bright and clean and shiny. They were fresh off the tree. The other girls' oranges were dusty and soft.

Their oranges had traveled
in trucks along bumpy
dry roads all the way
from the plantations
to the city.
Their oranges
had sat in the
sun in dirty
markets.
Their oranges
had been carried in open
baskets along smelly polluted roads. Their
oranges were small and orange-brown.

The girls' dresses were faded and torn.
Anna Hibiscus was as bright and clean and
shiny as her oranges. All the people who
stopped wanted the big bright oranges
from the well-dressed little girl. Anna sold
all her oranges. She filled up her basket
again and again and sold them all. The other
girls sold almost none that day.

Anna Hibiscus was so excited. As evening fell, she rushed back through the gate and into the house. The money was in her pocket, and her smile was bright and shining.

But when Anna's father and uncles came home from work, they looked worried.

"Something happen for those girls at the gate today. Some kind of trouble," the eldest uncle said. "That Angelina, she with no mother, no father, only sick brother at home. Angelina always smile. Today she cry."

"Is true," said Uncle Tunde. "And that small one with polio shrivel leg, who has to work morning and night for food. She crying too."

"Yes," said Anna's father. "And that one with twelve brother-sister, who father done die, why she so sad today?"

The big bright smile fell off Anna Hibiscus's face.

Grandfather was worried. What had happened to trouble the poor girls so? He went himself to the gate, but the girls had all gone.

Anna came and stood beside her grandfather. They looked at the yellow lights and the hustle of the city. Anna held out her hand. The coins were shining on her palm.

"What is this, Anna Hibiscus?" her grandfather asked.

"I sold our oranges, Grandfather," she whispered. "Now the girls have no money for food for their little brothers and sisters."

Anna started to cry. Grandfather looked up at the empty orange trees. He looked down at his crying granddaughter.

"People will be hungry tonight, Anna Hibiscus, because of what you have done."

Anna hid alone in her room and cried.

Early the next morning, Grandfather called her. "Come, Anna Hibiscus. Bring your basket."

Slowly Anna followed her grandfather to the gate. The girls were already there, desperate to sell their oranges and plantains.

"Today my granddaughter will work for you," Grandfather said. "Today she will collect oranges from the market and bring them here. You will not have to walk back and forth in the heat every time your basket is empty. Today you will be able to sell many, many oranges."

Grandfather led Anna Hibiscus along
the road to the market. It was a long way.
There was no shade; there was no cool
grass; there was no sidewalk. On one side
of Anna was the gutter, with its old green
stinking water. On the other side was the
traffic—loud horns blasting, engines roaring,
exhaust fumes belching. Anna Hibiscus and
her grandfather went slowly because they
were an old man and a small girl unused
to walking to market. All the other people
jostled and pushed past them. Sweat poured
down Anna's face and
into her eyes. Her throat
burned with dust
and car fumes.

At last they reached the place where
the market women haggled and shouted.
Grandfather led the way to the fruit sellers.
He filled Anna's basket with the best
oranges. The bright coins from yesterday
were still in Anna's pocket. She took them
out and gave them to the orange seller.
Grandfather nodded.

Back and forth they went. Back and forth.
Sweat stained Grandfather's shirt.
He leaned heavily on his cane.

Grandfather was too old to walk back and forth in the hot busy city.

"Maybe Mama or Auntie or Uncle could walk with me, Grandfather," Anna said.

"They are all busy with their work," Grandfather said. "I will not give them more."

Tears poured quietly down Anna Hibiscus's face.

When afternoon came, Grandfather went to rest and Grandmother joined Anna Hibiscus. Anna walked on and on, the heavy orange basket on her head. She did not stop. Not once.

When night fell, Grandfather was waiting for Anna at the gate. The girls were there too. Everybody had big smiles on their faces.

"This one small girl work hard-o!" the gate girls cried.

"Carry enough orange for all of us to sell plenty-plenty!"

"Well done-o! Well done!"

Grandfather led Anna Hibiscus into the compound. Her feet had blisters, her head was aching, and her legs were sore. Her ears were ringing from the car horns. Her throat and eyes were stinging with sweat and dust and fumes. But Anna was smiling too.

"Grandfather, send her work again-o!" called the girls.

Anna Hibiscus's grandfather laughed.

"Anytime she is bored of the quiet compound," he said, "anytime she is tired of the peace and the quiet . . . well, Anna Hibiscus now knows what it is to work hard!"

Sweet Snow

Anna Hibiscus lives in Africa. Amazing
Africa. In a country called Nigeria.

And because of this, Anna Hibiscus has
never once seen snow. More than anything
else in the entire world, Anna longs to set
her eyes, her feet, her hands, on snow.

Anna Hibiscus lives in a wonderful house
with many, many rooms and balconies and
staircases both inside and out. But more
wonderful than this, more wonderful than
anything else in the entire world, so Anna
thinks, is snow.

All day long, Anna Hibiscus plays in the garden around the house. A garden full of cool grass to lie on, beautiful trees to climb up, and lovely flowers to smell. The trees are full of sweet fruit, and the flowers are full of sweet nectar. But nothing can be sweet like snow, Anna has decided; nothing can be so cool.

Anna Hibiscus lives with her mother
and her father, her grandmother and her
grandfather, her aunties and her uncles,
her cousins and her brothers, Double
and Trouble. Anna Hibiscus's family
is so big she cannot count them all. But
nothing is more uncountable than snow,
Anna thinks.

One morning, in the amazing land of Africa, in the wonderful house with the wonderful garden, Anna Hibiscus woke up and her room was white. Floating white.

"SNOW!" shouted Anna.

Anna's cousins Chocolate and Angel woke up. Anna was waving her arms, and the breeze from the air conditioner that cools down the hot African air was floating white all about her. There were Double and Trouble sitting on the floor, feathers around their mouths, chewing Chocolate's pillow.

"Snowing feathers!" Angel cried, and she shook her pillow.

Now Anna Hibiscus could think of
nothing but snow. Snow! Snow! Snow!
She and her cousins played snowstorms
howling down hallways. They stormed
through the rooms until their mothers
chased them out into the garden.

Anna climbed the big mango tree, where her big boy cousins were sitting, eating mangoes.

"This one's sweet-o," shouted Anna, biting into a ripe one.

"But not sweet like snow-o. You agree, Cousin Benz? You agree, Cousin Wonderful? Nothing's sweet like snow!"

Anna Hibiscus talked on and on until the boy cousins shook the branches of the tree and she almost fell out.

She climbed down, shouting, "Just because you no know snow!"

It was true. Her cousins knew nothing about snow; her father knew nothing about snow; her grandfather and her grandmother knew nothing about snow; her aunties and her uncles knew nothing about snow; even Anna Hibiscus herself did not know snow. Nobody in Anna's family knew anything about snow because nobody in Anna's family had ever, even once, seen snow. Nobody except for Anna Hibiscus's mother.

You see, a long time ago, before Anna Hibiscus was born, when her father was a young man, he had gone to the land called Canada. He had gone in the short summertime, and there he had met Anna's mother.

They had gotten married and come quickly back to Africa before the long winter came and Anna's father got too cold.

So Anna's mother knew all about snow. She had been born during a snowstorm and had grown up building snowmen and throwing snowballs. She had sledded and tobogganed over mountains of snow. She had even skied

across snow-covered fields to school.

But Anna knew better than to ask about snow again, now, today, when her mother and the aunties were busy in the house.

So Anna Hibiscus went to the gate, but everybody outside was quick and shout and hurry today: buying and selling, haggling and arguing, walking and rushing; *quick* and *shout* and *hurry!* Nobody wanted to stop and talk to Anna except for a small beggar boy. Anna gave him the mango she had in her pocket. She started to tell him about snow—like cassava flakes falling from the sky!

"You de craze," the beggar boy said, and ran away.

"I no de craze!" Anna shouted.

She ran to tell Grandmother.

"It is not kind to talk of cassava falling from the sky to somebody who is always hungry," her grandmother said.

"You must be crazy, Anna!" whispered her cousin Chocolate.

Anna Hibiscus was cross. She went
into the kitchen. Uncle Bizi Sunday
would be there, and he would be nice
to her. He was the chief of the shopping
and the cooking. And he was often in the
kitchen, commanding and organizing it all.

When Anna Hibiscus came in, Uncle Bizi Sunday was measuring rice. Anna watched the small white grains being scooped up from the sack and falling into the bowl.

"Snow is like rice, Uncle," said Anna. She knew that he was not hungry. She knew he would not say she was crazy. "Like rice falling from the sky," she said.

Anna reached for some rice to show him how it could fall from the sky, but Uncle Bizi Sunday closed the sack.

"Finish," he said.

"Oh," said Anna Hibiscus. "Well, rice is not so much like snow. Snow is cold." She looked around and saw the big freezer. "Cold like ice," she said.

Anna Hibiscus opened the freezer. It was cold and soft inside. She scraped out handfuls of ice and threw them into the air.

"Look, Uncle!" she said. "Look at the snow!"

Ice flew into the air and fell onto the floor. It melted into puddles.

Uncle Bizi Sunday looked at the puddles. "Overseas is snow," he said.

"Yes, Uncle, in Scotland and Alaska and Iceland and Canada," said Anna Hibiscus.

"Snow dey for kitchen?" said Uncle Bizi Sunday.

"No, Uncle," said Anna slowly. "It snows outside."

"So why snow fall for this my kitchen?"
Uncle Bizi Sunday was aggravated.

Anna hurried to mop up the puddles.

Her mother came in while Anna was mopping.

"Anna! I have been looking for you," she said. "Here is a letter from Granny Canada! How would you like to visit her next summer? She will buy you a ticket on an airplane!"

Anna Hibiscus stood still as a stone. Only her eyes grew wider and wider.

Suddenly she leaped into the air and shrieked like a peacock.

"SNOW!"

Anna Hibiscus sang, waving the mop.

"Snow, you are wonderful!
I will see and tell you so!
Snow, you are so cold-o!
I will feel and say you so!
Snow, you are so sweet-o!
I will taste and tell you so!
SNOW—"

"Anna!" her mother interrupted gently. "There is no snow in the summertime."

Anna Hibiscus stopped dancing. Her eyes grew full of tears. Uncle Bizi Sunday came to stand beside her. "Dis child have to see snow," he said.

Somewhere inside the house, Double and Trouble started to cry. They cried and cried and cried. Nobody was picking them up.

Anna's mother turned to go. "I just don't know," she said.

Anna sat down on the floor, and her tears splash, splash, splashed into a puddle. Uncle Bizi Sunday hurried out of the kitchen. When he came back, he was carrying paper and an envelope. He took a pen from a drawer.

"Anna Hibiscus," he said. "Come! You must write."

"Why?" Anna wailed.

"You must write for Granny Canada— tell her you love snow."

Anna stopped crying. She looked at Uncle Bizi Sunday.

"Come," he said. "You write. I post."

Uncle Bizi Sunday wiped away Anna's tears and sat her on a stool to write.

Dear Granny Canada,
Thank you for inviting me.
I want to see you and Canada and
the bears and go on the airplane.
But I wish I could see snow too.
I really really really love snow.
Love from Anna Hibiscus

Anna put the letter in the envelope
and stuck it down.

"I no know address!" she wailed.

"I know it," Uncle Bizi Sunday said.
"Your mama told me one time."

Uncle Bizi Sunday had never been to
school. He could not read; he could not
write. But he could remember everything
he was told. Even if he only heard it
one time.

He said the address carefully and Anna copied it down. The letter was ready! Uncle Bizi Sunday readied himself. He took off his apron and put on his shirt. He put the letter in his pocket.

Anna Hibiscus watched him walk to the gate. She saw him stop and count the coins in his pocket before he went out. Then he was gone.

Anna Hibiscus waited while Uncle Bizi Sunday took the letter to the post office. Had she spelled the address right? Anna Hibiscus crossed her fingers. She waited a long, long time while the letter was sitting in the post office until an airplane flew it all the way across Africa and over the ocean to where her granny lived in Canada. She waited while the postman in Canada slowly read the address and then

delivered the letter
to her granny. She
waited while her
granny opened
the letter, read
it, and smiled.
She waited
while her
granny wrote a
letter back and that
new letter flew all the way
across the ocean and
all the way
across Africa
to where
Anna Hibiscus
lived. Anna
Hibiscus waited
for weeks for that
letter, while her fingers
remained crossed.

Then one day, as Anna was sitting in the
big mango tree with her cousins, somebody
shouted,
"A letter!
A letter
for Anna
Hibiscus!"

Anna almost fell
out of the tree again.
Everybody in Anna's family came
running. Her father, her grandfather,
her grandmother, her uncles, her aunties;
all of her cousins; her mother with her two

baby brothers; but first and fastest was
Uncle Bizi Sunday.

"A letter from Canada!" Chocolate
shouted, looking at the stamp. "Read, Anna!
Read!"

Dear Anna Hibiscus,

Why don't you come and visit me at Christmastime instead? Then there will be plenty of snow for you to see. I would love to have you to stay for Christmas. See what your parents say.
Love, Granny Canada

Anna Hibiscus took a deep breath. She looked up at her mother and her father. Her father was looking at her mother. Her mother was looking at her.

"Anna Hibiscus?" her mother said.

"I wrote to Granny Canada," Anna said. "I wrote that I love snow."

Her mother opened her mouth, but before she could speak: "Initiative!" said Grandfather. "Can she go?"

"Of course," her father said. "Of course you can go, Anna Hibiscus."

Anna could not move. Christmastime. Here the trees would be covered with leaves and lights and her family would be dancing to music beneath them. The days would be long and warm.

But she, Anna Hibiscus, would be where the trees were bare. The days would be short and cold and she would play in . . .

"SNOW!" shouted Anna.

Everybody cheered and clapped and laughed. Chocolate and Angel sang. Uncle Bizi Sunday danced Anna Hibiscus around and around. Hip, hip,

HOORAY!

"Snow, you are wonderful!
Anna will see and tell you so!
Snow, you are so cold-o!
Anna will feel and say you so!
Snow, you are so sweet-o!
Anna will taste and tell us so!
SNOW!"